IN RESPONSE

IN RESPONSE

CLAUDE MOORE

Parlyaree Press
Atlanta, Georgia
www.parlyaree.com

Library of Congress Cataloging-in-Publication Data
Names: Moore, Claude, author.
Title: In Response / Claude Moore
Description: First Edition | Atlanta : Parlyaree Press, 2023
Identifiers: LCCN: 2023908817 | ISBN 9781961206038 (paperback)
Subjects: LCGFT: Poetry
LC record available at https://lccn.loc.gov/

Design by Parlyaree Press

Front Cover/Title Typeface is Continuo by Delve Withrington from Delve Fonts & Avenir designed by Adrian Frutiger and released by Linotype GmbH. Glyphs from Espiritu, Cardo, Apple Symbols, and LTC Fleurons.
Cover Imagery (Pressed Pansies) Licensed from Adobe.
Interior Text Typeface is Clarendon URW from URW Type Foundry.

Print ISBN: 978-1-961206-03-8
Ebook ISBN: 978-1-961206-04-5

To myself, which may not be very couth,
but I've worked so hard to find me.

Table of Contents

Take, for instance, this:
That I am always on the precipice of finding
—Between searching and discovery—
And that I, for surely it can only be me,
Toss my words like petals—Evil Flowers[1], and
        French no doubt[2]—
Upon the path toward the cliffside,
Translated,
Where sinking and floating are the same.

---

[1]   In reference to *La Fleur du Mal* by Charles Beaudelaire.

[2]   "Pardon my French," for it is a language I can barely speak nor vaguely understand. Though, as I am Southern, the phrase takes on a new meaning. And, Boy, can I be profane.

What, you may ask, where you are me, for surely I am
the author of these words, is the average homosexual
to do when presented with your sophistry? It is to me
then, where I am still me, in all variations, to respond
as follows:

1.   Take it on the chin (though a boxer, I am not)
where idiom and history meet parlance appropriated
to a common tongue.
>   ⁂ Where tongue means exactly what it
>   sounds like.
>   ⁂ Where maws gape and welcome, are
>   hungry, and are filled.

2.   Take it on the chin where I am a boxer, where
I became one of necessity after bouts with wine-hued
words.
>   ⁂ Bob and weave.
>   ⁂ Weft.
>   ⁂ Wear it with the pride of a prism-healing
>   bruise.

Tell me, then, of the stealing of words. To take
something which has been forced outward—a vicious
gift, the naming of swords—and make it my own.

Faggot—for I am the beginning of the fire.
Dyke—for I hold all the waters of the world.

Fairy, Pansy, Poof, Tranny
HermAphrodite: the naming of Gods.

I do not pilfer what has been freely given. The names
cast upon me, this language, this life.

Should you then find displeasure in how I use what
I've been given? This language? This life?

Then that is all the more reason to persist, says I,
while taking soft another syllable from your lip.

Each poem is an argument with myself
Wherein I do not forgive myself the
Subtleties of a language meant
As container ⁂ To contain
For what other purpose could there be?
Furthermore, I do not grant myself
        —could never afford myself—
Such frivolities of conned text
Wine dark seas[1] before a color was formed
Or, not the color, but rather
The name for it. We all saw it there. We saw it.
We saw it. But it was something else
In your eye.

---

1   From Homer — used in the *Illiad* and the *Odyssey*. It has been noted that Homer did not have a word for the color blue. Or perhaps he could not see it (the color). Or perhaps the sea were a different color then. Or perhaps wine itself were blue then. Else, Homer meant unruly and drunk.

You erase me from your histories and ask why I am so new.

Men—for it is certainly nearly always men and a very particular type of coward—take their place as pallbearers on either side of what was, seeking interment (though often adding an errant "n"[1] when necessary).

Which camp will you fall in?

Where camp is high in performance, adding humor to a bit of meaning, and still containing multitudes.[2] Sing, then, a verse to create a newness that was always there. Call me out for my calling. For I hear myself in the parts you have buried. I have seen myself beneath the ashes of Pompeii. A seed well-preserved; a flower's death. A sprout.

---

1 In response to your "internment camps" where those othered or feared by society have long been placed.

2 Another bit of borrowed text (for how else could one respond?) from Walt Whitman - "Song of Myself"

Viscus

To follow ⁂ my gut

Viscous

To become ⁂ thick and heavy, both solid and not

Vicious

Too singular ⁂ when I is added and the
                                serpentine flow is removed

Viscera

To feel (again) in the gut

Visceral

To contain ⁂ on instinct, alone.

If I am to be
Where would you have me form?
Certainly not within the other(ed),
For some place so crude is not befitting a becoming
Become instead of the ocean
Where death lays cold in condensation, ringing
What was left in life before it could
Emerge

Tell me of your:

1.   Dialect

    ⁂ What forms around your tongue when you link it to your language?

    ⁂ When you twist your pronunciation, do the words fit better inside of you?

2.   Diphthong

    ⁂ String it together, that long moaning sound.

    ⁂ Let me hear it when you open wide. Say "boy."

    ⁂ Call me something cloying. Sweet. Yours.

3.   Jargon

    ⁂ Give me the language to speak to you as you'd like to be spoken to.

    ⁂ Tell me where argot turns to cant becomes can't survive without.

4.   Secrets

    ⁂ The watchword — peel it backward.[1]

    ⁂ Say it again and again until we are safe.

---

[1]   In response to "Cornflake Girl" by Tori Amos.

Autodidact

I get this wrong all the time—what else should I have expected?—for when asked if I carry myself to your grace, my answer is always a resounding yes. For what else could I answer when you are at once so effortless and so inspired. I pretend, in my own good grace, to not see the troubles you carry, placed into being beneath the carved balsa wood. Whittled, whitened, whistled down to the quick—two eyes, a nose, and a fast forked tongue.

Or else I am merry, secretly, for how else can I express true joy? Surely I am not meant to be Mary in public. To be met with such a bargain, however cleverly disguised, is not merely performative, so it can not—no, must not—be shown. These things you speak like rips in my apron, along the skin of my knees. Tear into me from just below the breast, cleave me in two. Slice until we are solid. Until all that is left is all that is whole. Each part now stands alone. Eager. We become polymaths, all of us together, each of us as one.

In response, I will speak to myself just loudly enough for you to hear, so that the whisper becomes the whole of what you see.

For everything I am is what I've taught myself to be.

An understatement (really, for that's all it could have been) when I said I understood. Understanding (as I did, but would argue you did not if I were inclined to be argumentative) such comprehension had little to do with what was being said. You liken me to Orpheus.[1] State: "A love like yours leads but one direction." Not realizing your understatement. Not knowing how much I love to travel down.

You placed your words in paradoxical slants. Aligning love with lust with hatred with sex. Telling me (demanding, really, for that's all it could have been) your love for my soul was what guided you. You liken me to Sisyphus.[2] State: "Fool me once..." Not realizing your thrice-bound ways. Not knowing I have always carried this weight.

---

1   In the Greek myth of Orpheus, he must survive the ascent from Hell without looking back at his love or his love will forever be trapped there.

2   In the Greek myth of Sisyphus, he tricks the gods thrice in defeating death and is punished to roll a boulder uphill for all eternity.

You (for it is always you who has to have the last word) use long-dead texts as justification. I (for it is always me who must hear beyond what you are saying, shovel through the false-hope toward your bitter-root) proclaim existence merely as it is. You liken me to Icarus.[3] State: "Your pride will get the better of you." Not realizing it is you who is burning. Not knowing it is you who is too close to the son.[4]

---

3   In the Greek myth of Icarus, he flies too close to the sun with wax-made wings. The wax melts and he plummets back to earth.

4   In the Christian myth of Jesus, "son" replaces "sun" replaces nature replaces soul.

He moved with a stuttering grace
If only imagined, as he shook
The debris of a winter left wanting
From his shoulders.
Never quite cold,
Though not really warm either, he
Was left in a meandering limbo.
Forced autumnal wanderlust
Desires run thin and compliant.

Emerge: lift out of the soil
Even in the downward push
Two slicked back tendrils
And Cassiopeia, unrivaled

Make it a mask to hide your true self. Your beauty will
Surface only when you ✬ want it to.

So then, does Poseidon enter
Make the waters his in as much as they were hers,
Are theirs

Which will you wear?
And which will matter most when
The roots are exposed?

My garden.
A bed of red clay. Tilled. Cleared. And loam added to
Enrich the flow of moisture.
To aide the roots in absorption.
Then I plant:

> Rosemary and basil.
>
> Lettuces (4 types).
>
> Okra which does not sprout.
> Too, Painted Ferns in the shade for their
> foliage. Sage. Yarrow
> (Flowering red and yellow both).
> Wormwood because I
> Like the taste of New Orleans on my tongue
> and
> I am nothing if not nostalgic.
> Fanciful. Fantasy-filled.

Then, I dig in Rhododendrons that ache like
Grandmothers. Native Azaleas. Rabbiteye. Marigolds
To Stave off pests. I water. I wait.
I watch this body of cultivated things
deemed beautiful—
Told sturdy and strong and eye catching and right
(And they are! Naturally. For how could they not be
When propagated from one so fine to start?)—

Droop under the sun. Beg. Thirst.
Even as the fresh-tilled soil sprouts what was
                    pulled out—
Clover and Crab Grass and Dandelions
          (all beautiful too, are they not?)—
Hungry for nothing more than light.
Then I know this is my body
Where all that is natural within will thrive
Despite what is placed upon it. Then I know
I should listen to the soil
When it tells me what it wants to be.

If we are to speak, let us speak in code
The kind that twin souls make
The type that skews off the page & moves far into the mar
Let it be a language only we can speak
One we decipher in accordance with
How we want the other to respond.

In this way, we will always get what
We hope to receive
Crows in nested pairs ⁂ wise in that way
The trinkets of lips which mean the world
(When that's what we want them to mean.)

I will receive your messages slowly
Take the time to savor them in my own
Interpretation
Interrupt them only when I need
A different word to mean the same

We can be gods in this way
In the mere act of creation.
We can get lost in this way
Isn't that what you said you wanted to begin with?

I will hear what you are saying
Make it holy
Give you meaning and worth and
Accordance

We can be joyful in this way

I will annotate[1] my words for you
Sometimes—when they are most obvious
And leave others for your codex, that secret ring
From the back of the cereal box
Your morning alive
In sugared possibility

---

1   Create footnotes for the evident. Create glimpses of the evidence. Give you a chance to unwind..

I was unaware then (and perhaps even now) that this was to be a competition. I stretch. Limber up. Push skin over ligaments. Feel (a filling up, really) the allegories you place on my body. Myths. But I can be mythic when prompted. That is the power of the homosexual. Our over-coming. Our pulse.

To you then I look for comparison. Do you possess an enjoyment of your own skin? Will you stretch. Limber up. Push skin over ligaments. Find (a filling up, really) that which you place upon yourself? An answer. A question. In the words of my namesake:

Tu n'as pourtant pas la prétention
d'être plus pédéraste[1] que moi?[2]

---

[1]   Though today we draw a distinction, when written Claude Cahun utilized the common word for homosexual.

[2]   "You surely don't have the pretense to claim to be more homosexual than I?" -Claude Cahun, *Aveux Non Avenus*.

Who are you, then, to make my body a political one

When I have been claiming but this all along:

Existence.

Govern-Nance

What is egalitarian about this? These bodies posed
in such positions: one, ready to enter; another to turn
his back. Perhaps a third (or fourth if I'm lucky) ready
to jump into the fray. Pulse together. Become worn.
Become warm. Become a warning. Then pass off into
the night--ships all along. No one getting what they
want.

Push forward. Find rapture where you ought to
find ecstasy. Find the two unequivocal and raw.
Whispered into handkerchiefs (let them do the
talking). But then, what was it you intended to say in
the first place? Could it have been as perfect as:

      1. Roses - No, red alone. Where it gets into
           the blood and finds a course of
           resistance.

      2. Lilies - Those which ornament the
           gravesides and wilt, turning grey
           before they are done, bound on all
           sides.

      3. Pansies.

You: who would take the universe to bed with you[1]—
Who me? Yes.
For in this instance: you are me. We can let it be but one
of the rare times we will coincide and leave it at that.
Merge, as it were, until we are both
Facing the same direction. Florid—flushed
And elaborate—
Heaving in the heavy nectar of sweat;
Legs intertwined. Turgid—versed
And well-spoken. (Who me?)
Combine, combine, combine. Wait
Until you hear me come.

---

1   "Tu mettrais l'univers entier dans ta ruelle" from Charles
Baudelaire's *Fleur du Mal*.

In response to no one in particular,
You invoke the gods.
You have brought this upon yourself, this asking
This need, this want. You say,
"Oh, gods." You say,
"Guide me." You say,
"Yes."

You take it upon yourself, this pleasure.
This seduction. This grip.
It is yours, but it's in gods' hands now. Ask,
"Can I?" Ask,
"Please?" Say,
"Yes."

I am not concerned with the cover of darkness for there is nothing I wish to hide. That shame should be placed upon someone, as a burden, would—of necessity—annul the obligation to carry such a load. For if it may be forced, it may also be denied. (The old Rubber Vs Glue argument.[1]) I alone will chose which loads I bear.

---

[1]   Though its origins are unclear, it is assumed by many that the case was first tried in Huntsville, Alabama and presided over by Mr. P.W. Herman.

Your breath, expedient in my ear, urging me onward with immoral tongue. I hear it all too well, even now. Now you have softened, retreated across mattress plains, topographical folds in fabric creating chasms. I hear it as you slow: inhale—exhale. I stroke as companion. Inhale=down; exhale=up. Again and again. Matching your breath. Inhale. Exhale. Inhale. Down. Up. Exhale. Go faster, I urge you. I urge your dream toward the cliffs. A bit of excitement to catch your lungs. My toe finds your skin beneath the covers.

Cruising

I watch Spring take hold in steady gallops, gallivanting through the trees like men do on Parkside nights. An unsteady folding ("lean into it") or, better still, a yearning (three taps on a window which may or may not move down). Color calls in muted bouts at first, then bursts—sturdy, nude and aching—into Buds. Bucks. Bungle down into the bushes. Sloppy and ham-fisted. Steady. Seeded. A rush of pollen and early evening air.

Bathroom Talk

Lights up on MARCUS, standing at the 2nd urinal from the LEFT. Awkward, alone, staring at the ceiling, at the "wall" in front of him. He taps his foot.

A second MAN enters, choosing the farthest urinal to the RIGHT. A third MAN enters, leaving a space between them all. The second MAN leaves. The third MAN leaves.

ELLIOTT enters and approaches a urinal.

A Beat.

MARCUS

You come here often?

ELLIOTT

I'm sorry?

MARCUS

I was just... Nothing. Nevermind.

ELIOTT finishes and goes to wash his hands. He looks back to MARCUS, still standing awkwardly at the urinal. He takes a step back toward him.

ELLIOTT

You alright there, man?

MARCUS

Me? Yeah, yeah....

ELLIOTT

I mean, I'm not gay or nothing, but... You know. If
you need help...

I am open to the idea, sometimes, that what I think
I see is sometimes something wholly other than the
thing that is actual. Actually there. What I mean by
sometimes is often-times. What I mean by *something*
is you. What I mean by *you* is one of those things
that is wholly other and extravagant; relatable;
misanthropically clever enough to surface when I
least expect it.

What I mean by *wholly*

is holy

is you.

Me: the heretic.

Heretically calling for your hearsay. Tell me: do they say I'm good after the act of evil?[1] When the worship is over, who do they proclaim as god?

Me: at their altar.

Altering, obviously, as one does, the binary. Up and down. In and out. Spit or swallow.

Am I now a god? Will they call me that when I am gone?[2] Will they make me the devil they always wanted me to be?

---

1   Their word, not mine. But I'll use it here. Hear it?
2   From the bed, from the backseat, from the bushes.

In an effort not to offend,[1] I should not describe their color. Except to say that in the highest of sun, their skin was rich and deep while in the midst of night they appeared pale and palid. For the light in between their parlor would run the gamut, dance joyfully within the queer space of inconsistent ingenuity.

In the forced fluorescent they would take on the artificial glow of fossil fuels. Of nuclear fission.

Do not take my coloring as a sign of theirs. Though they are my mother. My father. My other. My color, as it is, is quick to chameleon when it senses danger.

Take this for what it is. And for what it will be.

Too, they were slight of frame when the wind wswept eastward; full and heavy if it veered west. The north and south held little effect. The demi-cardinal gusts left their figure in flux.

---

1   Anyone who would be offended.

Glance sideways... Askew... Ask: Where should my hand go next?.. Know... You should know... It is not your hand I am seeking... Mouth... That's the stuff... Wet until it opens... Slide inside... Rest... Wait... Let the weight of it take hold... Let your body understand the stretch... Ask: Is that all you got?.. Answer: No... Move... Pulse... Quicken... Breathe when needed... Hold to make it last... Ask: Are you ready?.. Come... Go... Do not ask: Do you love me?

In response to your brutality
I write—an orgiastic pursuit—
All of my voices carving letters on a page
Our common tongue
Using, as I must, the words you have used against me
I take them in
Let my lips run over them in the way you like
Wet them, carve them down into
Something more palatable
So that you may see them formed:
Common ground—I offer—
An orgiastic pursuit if you be so inclined
Accept them as they are
And know I will not change

You giggle. Tell me, "You know the French call this *la petite mort*. The little death." You say, "Agony and ecstacy are so closely related." You say, "There's such a thin line between love and hate. Betwixt life and death."

I smile. I wipe the sweat from your brow. I know that inclination, that desire to make this more than it is. The need to make us holy. To make us limenal. To make us one. I say, "Then here we are. Let me try to kill you once more."

I have trained myself to listen to the edges of my throat, to that gasp of air around my words. I am tuned enough to know that sound, to hear it well and reasonably masked into the coattails of cadence, of lilt. The struggle of a body not meant for what the world has become. The rasp of a preliminary grief.

Primal.

Hollow.

It is (is it not?) the same sound I heard by the stream. Air grown louder than water. Breath denied under the circumstances. A floundering. A flopping. I carry such death when I speak so that you may know how close I am to escape.

Unlike your sister Air we claim you:

Solid. Stiff. Masculine. Firm.

Yet here you are, wet and softened from the shower.

Here you are: pushed through and divided

Realigned and reformed by the roots of

The living. Six feet of you displaced

By the dead.

(To be so malleable! Hard and unforgiving. Carved
through by the rush of liquid. Thirsty. I can be both
in simultaneity. Like you, I can contain what has died
to grow what will become.)

Open yourself to me... rupture... cleave what was there to make room for what I want you to be. Where? Here. From here to here. It only takes a moment to become hollow. I can show you how. (I've done it all before myself.) So simple a task. I wouldn't have you any other way.

From this you can take: solace, experience. All the things meant to allow humanity to present itself. Presents, really. What I give you. When I am gone, use the hole I leave behind to collect old coins, epistolary praises, stamps.

I will send you letters from: Beyond. An unknown place I have yet to travel. I will write expressively. In beauty. In rapture. And I will be vain enough to think my words will touch you where I once did. My effort, the least I could do, after your receiving.

If I am to understand you correctly,

I will need:

Flowers, attached still to the root, to the soil.

A flock of solitary songbirds. Bring them in flight.

The whole of your face as translator.

The image you tried to hide.

Gather these together as a spell. Spell it out so that
I may, correctly, understand your needs, your wants,
the base of your basest desires. Give them to me: the
cruel and unusual implementation of your own self
into disheveled dirt.

Do you keep your death folded gently into your pockets?
Where the tip sticks out just so, flagging
Left or Right
Do you carry it with you always?
That little notion of living, reversed
Ready. Ready.
It has, of necessity, become a part of you.
You keep it near as you switch between
          Acceptable.   Unruly.
Let it breathe. Let it hold its breath.
It is constant: this change.
Mourn not for me, you say. You say,
I have this held close so that I may always know
Rebirth.

I find it courageous, this wanting
Begging parts of myself to expand
Veer out into the world, show
And tell in neon pulsing lights.
It is my joy, you see,
These parts of me placed out
On display. Irrigated lands
Carved and teeming with honey.
I show you what I need
I need this, I say.
I invite you to my garden.
I want you there.
I let you cut me. Call it pruning.
I smile.

I am thirsty for regret. Parched, it would seem. Each new droplet of spittle on your lips sends my stomach to churn, ache, lunge, beg. Not always in that order. I think of what it would mean to taste your lips, neck, chest, cock. Always in that order. A ritual of romance where I bow down and rise. Reset. A thing we call romance because we find it better than the alternative. More palatable. With each new drop of spittle on your lips I can grow entire orchards. Trees: firm and rooted. Those which bear fruit and nectar and all of the sustenance I would have needed to begin with. A cycle, really, of life and death. You could water the fields for ages. Wet your lips. Reset the ritual to begin anew.

If all we do here constitutes gesture

When does:

1. My fist to your lip become movement?

2. My pen to your paper become moving?

You, for it was you, (was it not?) begged me for a warning.

Queen Anne's Lace.

Mugwort.

Cinnamon.

Cohosh.

Sage.

Pennyroyal.

Cotton Root.

Rue.

Possibilities I had not had to think of for my own body. I grow them now for yours. For who are we when our thoughts end in our own minds? Who would we be if our actions did not move?

I know (not in the sense of having been told) you want me dead. You ask for this timidly, as if embarassed by the implications, as if attempting to cleanse your skin of its blemish. You say: *not you but those like you.* You say: *that is not what I mean.* You decipher my humanity in actualities (not in the sense of having been told) in opposition to those you have yet to meet. Your alterity informs the core of your murder. Your site is set upon me. Whether you realize your aim or not.

You know (not in the sense of having been shown) the difference (so-called) in them (called so) but not in me where it is thriving even as you strangle it down.

I do not accept your acquiescence. Your words of war, that lickspittle of energy you use even while claiming majority, are evident even as you shy away from my being. I am every bit the homosexual you rile against. I know (in the sense of having experienced) the freedom of my life. I will not submit to your death. No. I do not submit to you.

I find your discomfort invigorating.

Isn't that so like me?

Should it not be? Afterall, it was already you who decided I was guilty. You who created these circumstances of my supposed being.

Should I not respond in my own justice? Should I not then be whom you have decided I am?

This is my lot in life.

Then I will take it upon myself. Revel in it. Rut my naked body into all of the corners of the word. Rip open the syllables until they are most comfortable in my maw. And smile.

If there is an opening

I will pursue the position voraciously.

Note them: the eager marks along my resumé.

The scribbles in the margins where

My pen has worked its method

Back and forth in descriptors I have given myself.

It is within all of this—this creation—that

I set myself up for success.

I am easy to work with, I say.[1]

Gentle. Observant.[2]

Ready to listen to your questions:

Let you call them prayers.

I can be distant and withholding, yes.

I learned that from the best of them.

Angry ✓ Vengeful ✓ Removed ✓

But also: Open.

I will open up, let you in, let you feel around.

I will do the job until I am deposed

To let another rise in my place.

Say, in all earnestness:

> God is Dead / Long live God

---

[1] "Easy to manipulate" is perhaps a better phrase here, for I can be silent while you tell others what I mean.

[2] Always watchful. But, again, willing to remain silent.

Je ne puis commettre les péchés d'un autre.[1]

I think often of this phrase. I revel in it. The ownership. The agency. The power. The humility.

It is humbling, is it not, to consider the very weight of being infallible. How I must carry it with these shoulders. And you, too, with your own. Though I see you have chosen to shame yourself in ways I have not.

That is your ability. Yours alone. For I am unable to commit your sins. And if our actions line up next to one another, form similar lines of touch and taste and sound, sweat together as oceans are formed. Bite. Breathe. Live. Die. If all of this happens as one, I still remain cleansed.

For what you call "sin" is your own.

I will never declare it mine.

---

1   "I cannot commit the sins of another." Claude Cahun. *Aveux non avenus.* Translated as "I cannot commit someone else's sins" by Susan de Muth in the English language edition *Disavowels.*

I am always so serious when I speak. This, your generous description of me, is accurate to a point. For you see, it is my duty—a privilege, really, you would try to convince me—to exemplify the rigorousness of humanity, of that very notion of being, when I am around you.

The code-switch of acceptance.

The cocksuredness of your own piety.

The "how to behave" of you to assuage the fears you have of my otherness.

It is due to this that you will never hear me laugh. You will not experience the joy of what true living is. At least not for me or my kin.[1]

But I do not see it as my own loss, this seriousness. I do not view it as my own hiding. Instead, it is a choice. I keep my love for those who would accept me as I am.

If I am always so serious, do you not believe you have simply gotten what you deserve?

---

1   Used here as kindred spirits. Chosen family.

Exquisite Corpse

You say it as if
The laying on of your hand(s)[1]
Does nothing more than to render
Lifeless that once-beautiful spark

It was a game, really
You said it was
At the house in Montparnasse
The Studio ⁜ Number 54[2]
Where all was decided
That powerful phrase
The reworking of my being

At least when you are done
What is left behind will be
Altered and exquisite
A composite of every hand I've touched

---

1   It is a ritual act, after all.
2   The Exquisite Corpse game, as invented by the surrealists, was first played at a home at 54 rue du Château in Montparnasse according to André Breton.

I do not complain (anymore) when you
Shut my fingers in the door
I see it (now) as only the minor inconvenience that it is
I have learned (finally) to be gracious
(Isn't that what you always wanted?)
To hold my tongue. Keep it firm and thick
In my mouth. Bitten through.
Who did I think I was (anyway)?
One worthy of admittance?
We both understand the price of admission
Is much too steep
And I would not be too comfortable there anyway
(Thank you, my friend, for deciding that for me
I never could have on my own)
I can admit it now
The safety of being shut out
Of making my own space, thumb throbbing
And bruised, but mine.

What?
You don't like that either?

It is a dangerous proposition, this new death being offered. I will take it. That is the polite thing to do. Let you shake me down to my bones—maybe singular, as it were. I can, of course, understand the desire. I am nothing if not benevolent.

So when Hades asks to take me into himself, should I not be Persephone? Should I not test the meter of his manhood? Should I not see where it can lead me? It is inevitable, is it not? This opening. This fulfillment. This murder.

That's what it is after all, a killing of sorts, no matter how you slice it. Even when I let you take me, I still feel the cut.

If I am to witness a new becoming
Please
Do not let the wind take my breath as it
So often does. Instead
Let what is natural ✣ inherent ✣ real
Guide us through to
Being.
In this way we can be christ-like
Turn water into wine—a natural process
Involving grapes.
And sun.
And time.

You call yourself the heterosexual. Say: I am the way of god. I, the homosexual, say: your language requires the Other in many ways. I list them: god v. man; master v. servant; other v. same. I go on and on. I speak but you do not listen. Perhaps my voice does not require another to be heard. So familiar with this dual collaboration, you find it commonplace; acceptable. Except where I am concerned.

As such, I grow concerned for you. Shrink. Stay back. Away. I, the homosexual, say: goodbye. Though I say it in opposition.

Ahh, but see: here is where we differ. Your writ of experience—what you call moral—has diverged from mine. I do not presume to make you like me, just as I do not assume your acceptance. My morality does not conflate information with persecution. As such, I do not attempt to place that on the other. What you take into yourself is not mine to control.

In so, I will open myself to great maws of possibility. A universe smiling. A universal understanding. Fibonnaci doing his sequences throughout all of eternity. Seeing the miracle in the natural. Seeing the god in the human touch.

And, once open, I will take it: dirt, shame, and seed. Grow. Sprout. Become all that your path did not allow for you to be. And I will urge you—in more ways than one, no doubt—perhaps this is your root—to tend to where you walk. To look back upon your path. To ask: Would this not be better with flowers?

Dance, they say.

Ask: how can I move when my limbs

Have atrophied?

Do not wait for response.

Drift. Swing.

A chariot will sway me if I ever

Refuse.

It was not up to me—this form; this growth. I took what I had been given. Created language around it. Disguised it as my own. Claimed ownership. Said: Mine.

Why then—and only then—were you to grow so jealous? Why then were you to decide my ownership would simply not do? Only once it was mine did you want it. Where was your attempt at control before I made it beautiful?

So then—and always now—I deny your attempts at possession. I am possessed enough of my own accord. My work shall be my own. I will enjoy the fruits of my self.

My postscripts are often longer than the letter itself.
For they contain
All of the subjects I meant to address before you
Were gone
And have only just considered in your absence.
In this way our correspondence has always been
Abbreviated. Shortened to a quick hand
An open viewing of interpretation
Even as the words lie still.

Acknowledgments

It should be another book, these acknowledgments, for I am humble enough—despite all evidence to the contrary—to understand the origin of my thoughts, of my words, and of my being is not within myself. I am an amalgamation of notions, feeding them through the basic reach of a language so vast and so finite.

As such, I will acknowledge you. And you. And you, you, you, and even you. I will whisper what you've taught me. Put pen to paper and hope I do it justice in passing it onward.

Claude Moore is a pseudonym. Claude Moore is an idea. Is a poet. Is an amalgamation. Claude Moore is a container—like a book in that way—broken open. Claude Moore uses they/them pronouns in respect of their namesakes who did not have that language, yet provided every nuance to the words.

This is their first book of poetry.

www.ingramcontent.com/pod-product-compliance
Lightning Source LLC
Chambersburg PA
CBHW010348220726
48290CB00016B/2684